THE ENJELLA™ ADVENTURE SERIES:
Storming Back to Key West

THE ENJELLA™ ADVENTURE SERIES: Storming Back to Key West

By Jane F. Collen

Illustrated by Peggy Davidson Post

Streamline Brand Associates, Inc.

Printed in the United States of America

First Edition: 2012

Print Edition ISBN 978-0-9855732-2-5

Visit www.Enjella.com for more information

To my (expanding) family: The Magic never stops.

Contents

A Fishy Story

SWOOSH!

SPLAT.

Abigail spit her toothpaste into the sink, turned off the water and ran back into the bedroom.

"I can't wait to fall asleep," she announced to her older brother as she bounced on the bed.

"You must be crazy," Bennett said, shaking his head, flying his Lego plane over her head. "I hate bed time."

"I have to see my Elbow Fairy," Abigail said.

"I guess that is why you are wearing your shoes to bed," Bennett said.

"Of course! Last night I went to the beach with Enjella so it was alright to be barefoot," said Abigail, tapping her head to indicate she was thinking logically, "but tonight, I am not sure where we are going, so I had better be prepared."

Bennett shook his head again. "Silly girl," he muttered looking at his electronic game.

"Wow," he said with surprise as he turned around to see Abigail brushing sand out of her bed.

"I guess I forgot to rinse my feet," she said, smiling at the memory.

"You really went to the beach? You weren't just dreaming?" he asked.

"Want to see my starfish?" she said.

"Itchy Ishkabibble!" Bennett shouted. "A starfish!" He could hardly believe his eyes. Abigail had a real live starfish floating in a little bit of ocean water in a beautiful bowl decorated with shells and seahorses.

"I just kept it for the day. Before we go anywhere else tonight, I have to bring him back and set him free in the tidal pool where he lives," Abigail announced.

"You are talking crazy," Bennett said firmly. Then he scratched his head. "Wait, it's the middle of January. Where did you really get a starfish?"

"I am telling you the truth," Abigail said as she put her hands on her hips and glared at him. "Why don't you believe me? Don't you remember Enjella? Our friend? The former Tooth Fairy? Now that she has started her own division of Fairies she comes to visit me almost every night. Last night she promised we would go back to the beach first, so I could return my starfish. After that we will be off on another adventure."

Bennett shook his head. "You are sticking to that story? Come on! Did you steal this starfish from the pet store or something?

"Tell me the truth, where did you really get it?"

"Why are you pretending I am not making any sense? How could you not remember Enjella? She came to visit us frequently. She even flew us both to her home in Sparkleshire. You met Her Majesty Jocelyn, Queen of the Tooth Fairies!"

Abigail shook her head. "I don't like this game! I am not going to argue with you! I will wake you up tonight when Enjella comes and you will see her again too," Abigail promised.

"This should be interesting! You are going to prove to me you got a starfish from a Fairy!" said Bennett.

"I won't say anything for now, but if I don't meet any Fairies tonight, in the morning I am going to tell Mom you stole a starfish!"

CHAPTER TWO

Sheepish Suspense

As soon as the children's mother called "TIME FOR BED" Abigail and Bennett jumped under their covers.

Their mother was amazed. "You never get ready this quickly! What is the joke?"

"Oh, it is not a trick," said Bennett. "We are just trying to make sure we get a good night sleep!"

"Now why don't I believe you?" their mother laughed. "Just don't do anything too silly," she said as she kissed them good night. "And don't stay awake talking and giggling too long!" She switched off the light and the florescent stars they had stuck to their ceiling glowed.

"Oooooo, stars," they both said automatically.

"No, starfish!" giggled Abigail.

"I love you, you Sillies!" said their mother and she closed the doors behind her.

Bennett leaned up on his elbow and looked over at Abigail lying in her bed. "When will she come? Do we have to go to sleep first?"

"Usually, I AM asleep, so I don't really know what time she comes," Abigail answered. "Maybe she is here already, and maybe she won't come until midnight!"

"Arrrg," Bennett rolled down off his elbow and flopped on his back. "It is going to be so hard to wait. I will NEVER be able to fall asleep."

"So you remember Enjella, and you believe me?" Abigail asked.

Bennett looked a little sheepish. Then he sat up tall and straight in his bed and tried to sound important. "No! I am just conducting an experiment. I am going along with your story to see where you really got that starfish."

"My Fairy held me by my elbows and flew me to a moonlit beach. It was warm and the sand was soft and squished between my toes! The ocean sparkled in the twinkling starlight," Abigail said dreamily. "And I found this beautiful starfish."

Bennett rolled his eyes and said, "Oh brother! Who could believe that? And hey! If I was going to invent a Fairy, it would not be an ELBOW Fairy. How did you come up with Elbow Fairy?"

"How could you not remember? Enjella got permission from Queen Jocelyn to start a new division of Fairies to help kids with ALL their problems, not just their teeth! I think they picked the name Elbow Fairies because they are always at your elbow whenever you need them.

"But if you don't believe in Enjella any more, why will it be so hard to fall asleep?" Abigail teased.

"I just like adventure," Bennett said. "And I am going to have an adventure finding out what you are up to!"

CHAPTER THREE

Is Seeing Believing?

ZZZZZZZZZZZZZ! Bennett was snoring! Abigail giggled softly to herself, and then she too fell asleep.

Suddenly a bright light glowed over Abigail's elbow. A soft fluttering sounded in her ear. Something tickled her nose and she woke up.

"Oh, it's you," Abigail said to the little sparkle of light in front of her eyes.

"I told you, I come almost every night," the tiny Fairy Enjella said. "But most of the children are asleep and never see me."

"That would be a good thing tonight, since you are wearing two different shoes!" Abigail said.

"Those are my good luck shoes," Enjella laughed. "I can sparkle through the sky faster when I am wearing them." She held up her foot to show Abigail the tiny wings attached to the back of each shoe.

Abigail smiled. "Well, even though they look a little silly, I like them! Thank you for waking me up. I did not want to miss our trip.

"My brother says he doesn't remember you! I have to wake him up so he believes me," Abigail jumped out of her bed and ran to Bennett's bed.

A stream of magic sparkling light shot out of Enjella's wand. The Fairy's magic picked her up by her elbows and gently flew her back to her bed. Abigail plopped down with her mouth open in surprise.

"Oh no, Abigail! He may be too old now to believe! In fact, boys can rarely see Fairies in the first place. It is a defense mechanism of the logical brain that he cannot remember me. Don't wake him up, he will never understand and he will only tease you."

"How can that be?" Abigail asked.

"Only children who believe in us can see us," Enjella explained.

Abigail looked confused. Enjella fluttered her wings. Her funny shoes sparkled and glowed. "I don't know why that is, exactly, it's just magic."

"Can't we just try to let him see you? I really want to prove you exist!"

Enjella shook her head, "Proving I exist is not the way to make him see me. He will have to look with his heart." She drew a sparkly heart in the air with her wand.

Abigail looked doubtful, but got up again to wake Bennett. She shook his shoulder and whispered, "She's here. Enjella the Elbow Fairy is here."

"And another thing," Bennett mumbled with his eyes still closed, "I would certainly remember if I ever met an ELBOW Fairy!" He blinked open his eyes and stared at Abigail. "WHHHHaaa?"

"Bennett, here's Enjella!" Abigail made a formal introduction.

Enjella sparkled and curtseyed. Bennett jumped out of bed and then just stared.

"Bennett," Abigail commanded. "Don't be rude! Say hello to Enjella."

Bennett rubbed his eyes. "You are crazy," he said, "you are talking to a little spark of light."

Abigail hung her head and dropped her hand in disappointment. But Enjella flew up straight in the air, setting off a rainbow of sparkles and landed on Abigail's shoulder. "That is great news, Abigail. The non-believers can't even see my sparkle."

Abigail cheered up a little, but said, "Well, now what do we do?"

Bennett said, "Go back to sleep, you dummy."

Enjella said, "I promised to return a starfish to his home tonight, if I recall correctly."

Abigail jumped up and clapped her hands. "Oh this will be so fun!"

"Going back to sleep will be so fun?" Bennett asked. He rolled his eyes. "You are definitely crazy."

"No, silly," Abigail said. "Going on an adventure with Enjella will be a blast."

"Are you still telling that story? No Fairy is going to visit us tonight. In fact, there is no such thing as a Fairy. You are talking to a little spark of light.

"But wait," Bennett paused and scratched his head. "How come that spark of light is still glowing? How do you do that?"

"I am not doing anything. This spark is Enjella. Maybe someday you will remember our adventures and be able to see her again," Abigail answered.

"You are going to have a little spark of light take you somewhere? How is that going to work?"

"Magic," Abigail said simply.

Bennett looked doubtful. "Well, but, even if I can't see her, and I can't figure it out, if you think you are going anywhere without me, you are even crazier than I thought."

Abigail turned to her little Fairy, "Can you take him too?" she asked.

Enjella looked thoughtful, "Technically," she said, "he is not one of my charges, so I can't." Abigail looked crestfallen.

"But YOU make the rules now! You are not part of the Tooth Fairy regime any more," Abigail begged.

Uncertain, Enjella flew back and forth as Abigail looked more and more disappointed. "Besides, he IS kind of big. I don't know if my wand has enough sparkle to fly BOTH of you to the beach, and then some…"

"Does Bennett have a Fairy that IS supposed to take care of him?" Abigail asked.

"Of course," Enjella replied. "All children do."

"If he has a different Fairy than you," Abigail said, thinking out loud, "maybe we can ask HER to come with us and fly Bennett. Do you know who she is?"

"Well, of course, and you do too! It's Alicia, my best friend! She helped me start the Elbow Fairies. Sometimes we even bump into each other here! I'll check her coordinates now." Enjella took out her iFairy and waved her wand over it. "Let's see…" she mumbled. "Enormous Elbows! What is the matter with this thing?" She shook her wand up and down and looked into the top.

"Hmmm," she said, as she tried again. "Oh, there she is. She is very close. In fact…"

Sizzle, sizzle POP!

A tiny bright light exploded into the room sending a cascade of rainbow sparkles up to the ceiling.

Hey," Bennett shouted. "It's a Fairy! I can see a little Fairy next to your spark of light."

"Wow," said Abigail.

She looked at Enjella and they both said at the same time, "He can see his Fairy!

CHAPTER FOUR

Spacesuits and Science

A little Fairy, who had green curly hair and was wearing a space suit, fluttered next to Bennett.

"You do not have to be so dramatic," Enjella said with a shake of her wings.

"I love a GRAND entrance," shouted Alicia, Bennett's Fairy, fireworks shooting from her green hair and reflecting on her sliver space suit. "Besides, I know Bennett likes fireworks and space ships, so I wear a sparkling space look in case of a face-to-face meeting!"

Bennett's mouth was still open with surprise. "How did you know I like space ships? What else do you know about me? How long have you been my Fairy?

"Whoa, slow down buddy! We have all night to get caught up and reminisce about our past!" said Alicia, and she slapped him on his back, with her wand, affectionately.

Bam! A shower of sparkles went up in the air and Bennett suddenly disappeared. In his place was a frog.

Abigail gasped. Alicia's hair turned red. Enjella shouted, "Alicia, pay attention!"

"Ooops," Alicia giggled. She zapped him again and up popped Bennett, with his tongue sticking out. Enjella glared at Alicia.

"Sor-ry," said Alicia. Her hair turned back to green as Bennett sucked his tongue in, just before a fly landed on it.

"UGGH," said Bennett and Abigail.

"Ishkabibble!" said Bennett. "I remember! We flew to Sparkleshire and I got turned into a giant! . . . How did you do that anyway?"

"You have been studying science in school, right?" Alicia asked, as safety goggles appeared over her eyes and a steaming smoking beaker appeared in her hand.

"Yes!" said Bennett, "and I have been doing a lot of extra reading. Of course! There must be a scientific explanation.

"Now, naturally, my original theory was that Abigail and I are asleep and one of us is dreaming. OOOUCH," he shouted and pulled his arm back from where Alicia had zapped it with her wand. "What the heck did you hurt me for?" he said, rubbing a bright red spot.

"Aren't you supposed to pinch yourself awake if you think you are dreaming?" Alicia asked. "I just saved you the trouble by simulating a pinch with my wand."

"I said that was my ORIGINAL theory, when I did not remember our previous adventures. I already disproved that one because I already pinched myself when I first saw you." Bennett started to pace back and forth between the two beds. "And I felt the fly land on my arm, so I am not asleep. And it could not be Abigail's dream, because I would not be able to think and feel in HER dream. SOOOOO...."

"Enough with the theories!" Alicia snapped, beaker and goggles disappearing and angry sparks shooting from her hair, "You will not be able to figure out how we do this scientifically, because there is no scientific explanation."

"It's magic!" both the Fairies and Abigail shouted together.

Abigail picked up her beautiful bowl with the starfish, "I am ready, let's go!"

"Finally!" said Enjella. She twinkled over to Alicia, "Now, no funny stuff," she whispered.

"Who me?" Alicia asked innocently, polishing her wand on her sleeve, "Whatever do you mean?"

Alicia's hair turned an efficient navy blue and she zoomed over to Bennett.

Enjella did not bother answering. She sparkled over to Abigail, touched her elbow with her wand, and they were off in a twinkle.

Bennett's mouth dropped open again in surprise when Abigail disappeared. "Hey, now what are you Elbow Fairies up to? I am too old to believe in..." Bennett's mouth snapped shut suddenly in mid sentence when Alicia, his Elbow Fairy, wooooshed him off into the night.

CHAPTER FIVE

Moonlight Mischief

Time and space seemed to warp in a funny way, Bennett thought, as they flew. They arrived at a warm moonlit beach in just seconds. But it was nowhere that Bennett had ever been.

"Where are we?" he asked.

"The same beach as last night," Abigail answered. "I think we are somewhere in Florida."

"Yes," Enjella chimed in. Both Fairies had stars shining in their hair and their eyes looked like moonbeams. Their clothing had turned to long dresses covered with moons and stars. "We are in Key West, the southern most island off the tip of Florida."

The warm breeze ruffled the children's hair. Abigail sniffed the air to enjoy the fresh scent of salt water. The Fairies now had fish and sea horses shimmering and swimming all over their dresses. Their hair looked more green-blue now, like the color of the ocean. And some of the stars were shooting off the tops of their heads.

Abigail sat down and took off her shoes. Enjella tapped the shoes with her wand, shrank them to doll size and put them in her Fairy pouch. Bennett and Abigail ran to the tidal pools with the Fairies flying behind them. The starfish jumped out of Abigail's bowl to be reunited with his natural habitat.

The water in the tidal pool sparkled in the moonlight. The children could see crabs scuttling to and fro, around and under the rocks. They leaned closer and closer to the water to count the starfish, the sand dollars, the mussels and the snails clinging to the rocks.

Splash!

Bennett tumbled head over heels into the water!

He pulled himself up, sputtering.

"Hey," he shouted at Alicia's laughing, twinkling, fluttering form, "you pushed me!"

"Who me?" said the Fairy, turning all shimmery and looking very innocent. "It could not have been me, I am way over here," she pointed her wand and a big arrow appeared over her head, flashing and pointing to her, "and YOU are over there!" The arrow streamed across the sky and pointed and flashed over Bennett's head.

"Of course, sometimes my wand seems to have a mind of its own…" Alicia's wand bent in two and took a bow.

Enjella shook her head disapprovingly, her hair turning a scary, threatening black. But then she smiled, in spite of herself, her hair returning to its sea foam green. The whole group, including Bennett, could not resist chuckling at the sight of a starfish streaming down his wet clothes and splashing noisily back into the tidal pool.

"I wonder if that was MY starfish?" Abigail asked as she helped to pull Bennett back up onto the big rock on which they had been kneeling. "Oh, now you will be all wet and dripping for the rest of our trip," she said in dismay.

"That is not a problem when you have magic at the tip of your elbow," said Alicia. She zipped up to Bennett and zapped his elbow with her wand. Sparkles flew out of one of the star points and streamed over the boy. He was instantly dry, but wearing a fancy shirt and tie instead of his pajama shirt.

"Why am I wearing this stupid tie?" he complained. "I hate ties."

"I just think boys look so nice when they are all dressed up," Alicia said, suddenly dressed in a very pretty party dress with fancy black shoes.

"Well, sure," said Abigail, "but that striped shirt and checkered tie do not go with his pajama bottoms!"

"Gotcha," said Alicia and she zapped him some new pajama bottoms in a crazy pattern of both stripes and checks.

"Oh, enough silliness," commanded Enjella with a quick SNAP of her wings. "Let's go!" She touched Abigail's elbow. Instantly they were transported to the nearby Key West Lighthouse.

CHAPTER SIX

Fairy Flights

"What are we doing here?" asked Abigail.

Enjella smiled. Beams of light seemed to sweep from the top of her head. "You will see," she said mysteriously, just as Bennett and Alicia materialized next to them.

"Ishkabibble!" shouted Bennett. "I love flying. Tomorrow night I am wearing goggles though. I get too many bugs in my eyes." He wiped his eyes with his tie and his nose on his already grungy sleeve. Black specks of bugs dirtied it even more. "I take it back! This tie comes in handy!"

Abigail and Enjella both made a face. Enjella's hair uncurled and became a sickly yellow in distaste.

Alicia zapped Bennett with her wand and goggles immediately appeared on his face. She flew back and looked at him. "How is that?"

"Great! These will work perfectly!" he said.

"No they won't," Abigail disagreed. "You look ridiculous. You will attract even more bugs as we fly, because now you LOOK like a bug."

Bennett stuck out his tongue as if to catch a fly on it. Alicia reached out her wand and zapped him back into a frog.

Abigail said, "Hey, wait a minute!"

Enjella turned around and saw Bennett the frog. She frowned. A thundercloud appeared over her head.

"Keep your wings on!" Alicia giggled and zapped him back into a boy. Bennett's eyes bugged out; he shook himself and shouted, "Cool!"

"Enough," said Enjella. "Tonight we are here to see a what a lighthouse does. If you will observe. . ."

"Who needs lighthouses anymore?" interrupted Bennett.

"That's not polite, Bennett," said Abigail.

Enjella gave him the evil eye as another eye appeared in the middle of her forehead and glared at him. She put her hands on her hips. "In days gone by, lighthouses were essential! They kept people and cargo moving by providing ship captains with critical information." Enjella paused and the beam of light emanating from her head landed on Bennett and stayed there. "You are right, lighthouses are not as important as they once were when the main mode of transportation was by boat . . ."

"Or since they invented radar, so a ship's navigator can see the layout of the entire shore, not just the rocks," said Bennett, proud of his scientific knowledge.

Alicia zipped in front of Bennett and screeched to a stop as a graduation cap appeared on his head. "Has everyone met this genius? That's right, I am his Fairy! I am in charge. Yes! I taught him everything he knows!"

"How do teachers do it?" Enjella muttered to herself. Out loud she said, "Thank you for your input: some of it helpful and some of it NOT." She glared at Alicia. "Might I be allowed to continue? Lighthouses still serve an important function; some are still active and protect small craft without radar and others . . ."

"Look scenic?" interrupted Abigail.

Alicia rolled her eyes and flew up to Enjella's ear. She circled them in a whirlwind of stars so Bennett and Abigail could not hear. "We can't compete with school teachers! I don't know how to explain the lesson this lighthouse teaches, we have to let them experience it!"

Alicia stopped the star wind and shouted, "To September 13, 1835, 3pm" and tapped Bennett's elbow, before Enjella could even say, "Mighty Magic – NOOOOOO!"

"Where did they go?" Abigail asked as Enjella snapped back her wings and zapped her elbow too. The words sounded in the air behind them as they somehow zoomed backward. She closed her eyes tight.

"It's ok, we are here," giggled Bennett, right next to her. Abigail opened her eyes and saw she was still standing at the base of the Key West Lighthouse. The sun was shining so brightly the glare hurt her eyes.

"Where is here?" she said in confusion. "Did we go anywhere? Why does the lighthouse look smaller?"

"Not any WHERE," laughed Alicia, "We went some WHEN."

"Now wait a minute," said Bennett, scratching his head. "How is that possible?"

"Oh Bennett, how is it any less possible to have Fairies fly us to a different time than to fly us to Florida in the first place?" Abigail asked.

"Well, I suppose you have some logic there," Bennett admitted. Then he jumped up in the air and shouted, "Itchy Ishkabibble, now I am thinking crazy too!"

"You are not thinking crazily," said Enjella with a smile, "just magically!"

CHAPTER SEVEN

A Woman's Work

"Glad to see that smile," Alicia said behind her wand to Bennett, her hair turning gold with relief, "I thought I was going to be in trouble!"

"You ARE in trouble!" said Enjella, her hair suddenly pulled back severely from her face and a police officer's hat appearing on her head, "but I won't read you the rules right now; since we came all the way back here, we might as well see the reason for our journey."

She snapped back her wings, and her clothes changed to an airline attendant's uniform. "Ladies and Gentlemen, we have arrived at our destination. We have gone back in time to the original Key West Lighthouse built in 1825. Welcome to September 13, 1835."

"Why did we come here?" asked Abigail.

"Don't you mean, 'why did we come now'?" asked Bennett.

But Enjella did not answer. She and Alicia each grabbed a child's elbow and flew them to the top of the lighthouse. When they landed on the deck circling the big lanterns, Bennett noticed the glare of the sun seemed to dim a bit as some big cumulous clouds moved overhead.

"I think a storm's coming," he said, just as a big rumble of thunder made them all fly up into the air.

"Yes, this is the beginning of the terrible hurricane in 1835 when, if it wasn't for the lighthouse…" said Enjella.

"Don't TELL them!" said Alicia. "We did not fly all the way back in time to TELL them what happened. We get to watch!"

Just at that moment, a bright blue bonnet appeared at the top of the spiral staircase inside the window, followed by a friendly face. A lady's brisk figure bustled up the stairs, wearing a long blue dress, and walked into the room at the top of the lighthouse where the lanterns stood.

Before Bennett and Abigail could blink an eye, Enjella waived her wand and made them invisible.

The woman, however, was so engrossed in what she was doing she would not have noticed them anyway. She immediately started the maintenance and cleaning of the 15 lamps. One by one, each of the lanterns was extinguished. As she waited for them to cool, she quickly cleaned the inside of the huge panels of glass encasing the room that housed the lanterns.

"Thaddeus, Thaddeus," she called as she reached in her apron pocket and pulled out a clean rag. "Why have you not minded me? I asked you and your brother Zachary to help me today.

"My goodness, gracious, but this heat is unbearable," she muttered to herself. Raising her voice again she shouted, "I am waiting for you boys to help me with the chores."

A screen door below them slammed. The Fairy team saw two boys run out of the cottage adjacent to the lighthouse, playing tag.

Mrs. Mabrity stopped for just a moment to take off her bonnet and brush her hair away from her hot, perspiring face. Then she briskly began to clean and polish the huge silver reflectors, which magnified the light of the lanterns.

"Wow! Running a lighthouse without electricity is an awful lot of work," said Bennett.

"Hey boy! WHISPER!" whispered Alicia. "You are invisible, not inaudible."

"What's inaudible?" whispered Abigail.

"SHHHHH," said Enjella, "it means Barbara can hear you."

"Who is Barbara?" whispered Abigail.

"Through this thick glass?" said Bennett.

"That is Mrs. Barbara Mabrity. She is the lighthouse keeper," explained Enjella.

"Wow, a lady is in charge?" said Abigail.

"Yes-sir-ee," said Alicia and banners that said 'VOTES FOR WOMEN' appeared on her hair and across her dress, "even though it was almost 200 years ago, a woman was in charge of this lighthouse! And because she did her job so well, thousands of ships made it safely past those dangerous reefs."

Bennett looked out over the lighthouse deck railing, "Whoa! Look at those waves! They are really hammering those rocks."

Alicia waved her wand and a pair of binoculars appeared. "The reefs are really taking a beating." Eggbeaters appeared in her hair.

"Can I see?" Abigail asked. She grabbed the tiny Fairy binoculars that magically grew to human size. As soon as she looked at the waves she shivered in fright. "I would hate to be on a ship out there in those dangerous seas.

"Oh no! There IS a ship, RIGHT there, heading toward shore," she pointed toward a spot in the churning ocean.

Bennett grabbed the binoculars. "I don't see anything but rough waters. There are waves crashing every where."

"Ugh a bug!" shouted Abigail, forgetting she had to be quiet.

"SHHH," said both Fairies without tearing their eyes from the little Fairy-sized binoculars they were using to stare out into the ocean.

"No, 'ugh,' a million bugs!" shouted Bennett. They temporarily forgot about the crashing waves and looked at amazement as Mrs. Mabrity swept millions of bugs out of each of the fifteen big lanterns.

"That happens every night," Enjella said over her shoulder to the children, her eyes still glued to the binoculars.

"That is correct," confirmed Alicia, her voice turning teacherly and stern, ignoring the fly swatters that dangled from her hair, "Every night millions of bugs, moths and other insects, attracted by the incredibly powerful light, are lured to their death by getting too close to the lighthouse lanterns' flames."

"UGGH," repeated Abigail, a little softer this time, absentmindedly wiping the sweat from her forehead.

Mrs. Mabrity was now outside the glass, on the balcony next to them, cleaning the salt spray off the outside of the lantern windows.

"Thaddeus! Zachary! I feel a storm approaching. It is the only thing that can break this horrible heat. Come now children, we must batten down the hatches."

ZAAAP! The children and the Fairies were inside the glass staring at the cooling lanterns.

"Each night, the powerful ocean assaults the lantern windows and leaves a film of salt which must be cleaned every day by the lighthouse keeper," continued the Fairy teacher as if nothing had happened.

"I thought we were going to let them experience the hurricane, and not give them a lecture," said Enjella, question marks appearing over her head.

"True," said Alicia, turning true-blue. "However, I want to set the stage for the drama to come." Her hair started to sizzle and a thunderbolt shot across her forehead. "Good ole reliable, hardworking, Mrs. Mabrity becomes the heroine of the hurricane!"

Fireworks burst from the top of Alicia's hair and cascaded over her shoulders.

"It's so hot," said Bennett, rolling up his sleeves and loosening his tie, looking outside at the two boys still playing on the rocks in front of the lighthouse wielding long sticks as swords. "When is it going to cool off?"

"Hurricane?" squeaked Abigail. She gulped the air. "Are we really going to be here for a hurricane?"

CHAPTER EIGHT

Fast Forward

"Do not be alarmed," said Enjella, as she ZAPPED the group back outside the big glass windows and patted Abigail's shoulder with her tiny Fairy hand. "We will not be in danger."

"Awww, that takes some of the fun out of it," said Bennett. He looked down over the railing at the stormy sea.

"Not to worry," reassured Alicia with a mischievous grin, red lights blinking in her hair, "the people we will be watching will be in very grave danger, and a little of that could always spill over and ensnare us."

A big wave crashed on the rocks just below them. The water sprayed so far up the side of the lighthouse they all got wet.

"Gee, thanks," said Bennett. "I needed some help cooling off."

"This is getting scary," whined Abigail.

"That was just an erratic wave," said Enjella briskly, looking at the pocket watch in her hand. "The serious storm is a long way off. Alicia, I suggest we fast forward just a bit."

Alicia gave Enjella the WINGS UP sign. The Fairies touched each child's elbows with their wands and a scrabbling noise was heard. Suddenly it was much darker and the sound of the crashing waves was deafening.

"Aye," cried Alicia, holding an old fashioned telescope up to her eye, wearing a Captain's hat, "the air is full of water, the water full of sound and no man can look windward for a second!"

"Huh?" said Bennett.

"Is this the dead of night?" asked Abigail in a small voice, which was carried to their ears by the wind, "I can't see anything, even if I don't look into the wind."

"No," answered Enjella, "it is ten o'clock in the morning, the day after we first arrived. The eye of the hurricane is only 30 miles away. Mrs. Mabrity and her family don't yet know, but it is due to pass directly overhead. That means the violence of the storm is just beginning."

Abigail shivered.

"Is the wind making you cold?" whispered Enjella. She winked at Alicia and they zapped the children on the elbows.

POP! The fairy team was inside the huge glass of the lighthouse, sheltered from the wind.

Mrs. Mabrity suddenly loomed out of the darkness from the top of the stairwell, heading straight toward them. Abigail gave a little cry of surprise but since the wind outside was so loud and they were invisible, Mrs. Mabrity just rushed right by them without stopping. She immediately got to work, removing the glass surrounding a lantern.

Her hands did not stop for a second as she called over her shoulder to two of her children. "Bring the rags, we must clean the lenses as best we can." The wind whipped her skirts, even though she was inside the windows surrounding the lanterns.

"Heavens to Murgatroid, what is keeping me bairns?" muttered Mrs. Mabrity. "I always mourn the loss of my dear husband John, but it's times like these, when I recall us working together to keep the light going, that I miss him most acutely."

"Mrs. Mabrity started her career as an assistant to her husband John." Enjella whispered this explanation to the children. "They tended the Lighthouse here together for almost 10 years before he died of yellow fever, about three years ago. The Collector of Customs immediately appointed Mrs. Mabrity as her husband's successor, based on her many years record of hard work."

"See how the wicks in the lantern are black?" Enjella turned their worried eyes back towards the lanterns. "That means they can no longer effectively burn the whale oil. The lanterns are going to start billowing smoke, the lights will dim and then burn out!"

"Mrs. Mabrity needs to get cracking on trimming those wicks," said Alicia wicks sticking out of the top of her head. "She does not have time to chase after her children. The boys need to get the whale oil up here to refill the lanterns before the lights go out completely."

Bennett turned his head towards the sand dune below. Immediately infrared goggles fell into place over his eyes.

"The boys seem to be arguing about something," he reported. "There are two big buckets just sitting in the sand and neither boy is picking them up."

"Oh no," cried Abigail, looking through her infrared goggles, "one boy just threw a punch at the other! They are never going to cooperate and get the whale oil up here to Mrs. Mabrity!"

"We'll just see about that," said Enjella. "Alicia, fly Bennett down there to the boys and see what you can do to get them and the oil moving up here."

Alicia gave the WINGS UP sign. She and Bennett were gone in a flash of lightening.

"Abigail, how are you at cleaning windows?" asked Enjella.

"I am not sure. I want to help but these windows are huge," Abigail looked them up and down in wonder.

"Size is relative!" Enjella's wand tapped Abigail to three times her regular size.

"I am now a giant!" said Abigail, looking at her hands in amazement. Then she looked back at the window and shook her head. "But these window are STILL huge!"

"How else would the ships, far out in the sea, be able to see the beacon of light?" Enjella smiled reassuringly. "How about some wings too?"

ZAAP! Abigail fluttered her new wings in appreciation.

"I am going to teach you how to use a little elbow grease!" Enjella fluttered her wings back.

"Who better to teach that than the Elbow Fairy!" laughed Abigail.

Enjella zapped herself almost as large as Abigail. She tapped her wand on her other hand and two chamois cloths appeared. They both immediately turned and started to clean the enormous windows of the lighthouse.

CHAPTER NINE

Minimal Magic

The soot soon disappeared as Enjella and Abigail scrubbed with all their might. They flew up and down the massive glass. Enjella tapped their cloths and the chamois rinsed themselves and wrung themselves out! They moved on to the next window as they saw Mrs. Mabrity still struggling to take each lantern apart, one at a time, and clean every piece of it, including the lantern cover and the magnifying glass. She was so engrossed in her task she did not notice that the windows were becoming clean!

Meanwhile Bennett and Alicia were standing at the base of the lighthouse scratching their heads trying to figure out how to help the boys resolve their differences and get that oil up the stairs.

"Its too heavy for me," the younger one was shouting. "I can't carry that huge bucket up all those stairs. Ma usually carries it up. What is wrong with her? Why can't she come down to help?"

"Thaddeus, you have to try! I can't carry two buckets. I can barely get one up the stairs."

"Why don't you make two trips?" argued Thaddeus.

"We don't have enough time!" shouted Zachary. "The lamps are going to run out of oil. If they are all burned out at the same time in a storm like this, a ship could be dashed upon the reef in minutes!"

"Alicia we have to do something!" whispered Bennett.

"No shine, Sherlock," said Alicia. A Sherlock Holmes detective hat appeared on her head. "But what?"

"You have the magic, think of something!" said Bennett.

"This here is what we call a real 'wand stumper'! I'll be star-struck if I know what to do. I am not allowed to fill the oil lamps by using magic; it is against the Universal Fairy code. I can't even zap the oil up the steep winding staircase to get it to Mrs. Mabrity," Alicia scratched her head under her Sherlock Holmes detective hat and mumbled, "some complicated mumbo jumbo about interfering with past events et cetera, et cetera."

Alicia's hair was green with worry and sticking straight out from her head as if her brain was working so hard and creating so much energy that her hair was forced right off its top.

"Well," said Bennett slowly, "If you can't use magic at all, we are really sunk."

"Not as sunk as that ship is going to be, out there tossing and turning in the turbulent waves," replied Alicia, as lifesavers now appeared on her head dangling from the ends of her hair. "But I am allowed to use SOME magic; I just can't think what will help."

"Wait, can't I carry up the oil?" he asked, as one boy jumped on top of the other, they tussled and started rolling down the hill in the rain.

"Certainly, but you can't carry both of those heavy buckets. And I am way to small to help," said Alicia.

"Small! That's it!" shouted Bennett. "You can shrink the buckets so I can carry them up the stairs!"

"Done!" cried Alicia, and smacked him on the head with her wand in joy. Bennett turned into a frog again.

"Grebbit," said Bennett.

"Magical Mishaps," mumbled Alicia looking at the top of her wand, "is this thing stuck on that spell?" She whacked him again and Bennett returned to his regular human self. She flashed around and shrank the buckets to drinking glass size before Bennett could say "Enchanted Elbows".

Bennett picked up both the buckets and climbed up the sand dune to the lighthouse tower.

Thaddeus and Zachary were struggling to their feet.

"Do you see twinkling stars?" Thaddeus asked Zachary.

"I can ONLY see twinkling stars," muttered Zachary, rubbing his head and still trying to regain his feet.

"Where are the buckets?" asked Thaddeus.

"I can't see anything! It is pitch black and there is rain in my eyes," said Zachary.

The boys looked around in the sand. A bolt of lightening struck a tree behind them and in the noise and commotion of the falling tree limb the tiny buckets were visible, floating toward the lighthouse.

"Do you see that?" said Thaddeus. "The buckets have become miniature and they are moving themselves to the lighthouse!"

"You've gone crackers," said Zachary.

"Follow me!" commanded Thaddeus. And he ran off in the general direction of the buckets with Zachary close behind.

Alicia was encouraging Bennett up the stairs, for even though the buckets were small, they were still filled to the brim and the circular staircase was steep and wound precariously around the inner core of the brick lighthouse.

"Steady now, Bennett, steady," Alicia encouraged, trying to support his elbow with her wand.

Bennett was huffing and puffing from the physical exertion.

"Watch your step!" warned Alicia right in his ear as she buzzed up the stairs next to him.

"I can't see the step any more," Bennett complained. "My infrared night goggles slipped off my face."

Alicia zapped them back on his face and secured them. Bennett slowly kept up his climb.

"Deep breaths," commanded Alicia. "Pace yourself."

Behind them they could hear the two boys, arguing again.

Suddenly it was even darker than before. Bennett and Alicia looked up the stairwell.

There was no longer any light coming from the top of the lighthouse!

CHAPTER TEN

S.O.S. (Save Our Ship)

"Hurry," urged Alicia, zipping back and forth in front of Bennett as he cautiously lifted his foot to the next step.

"Sure, its easy for you, you're flying," muttered Bennett, "I wish I had wings."

Wings appeared flying all over Alicia's hair.

"Why didn't you say so?" she asked.

She tapped a wing on each of Bennett's shoulder blades.

He zipped up the rest of the stairs in less than thirty seconds!

Enjella and Abigail were now frantically flying up and down the huge silver refractors trying to clean the dark grimy soot that still seemed to cover half of the light reflectors and mirrors.

They looked enormous to Bennett; the huge glass of the lantern magnified the enlarged Abigail even bigger. If he had not been so anxious to get the light restarted he would have laughed at the sight of the gigantic (yet invisible to Mrs. Mabrity) Fairy and girl sweating, scrubbing and scrambling to clean the glass.

Mrs. Mabrity was anxiously dumping old whale oil, full of soot and debris, through a filter into a bucket. She turned with a whirl and yanked old wicks from each of the lanterns; cutting off the dirty used up part

from the wicks that were long enough to last through the storm and re-placing the spent wicks in the rest of the lanterns.

A crack of lightening and a cry from Mrs. Mabrity cut short Enjella and Abigail's joy at seeing Alicia and Bennett and the little barrels of whale oil. They all turned to look at what caused her renewed horror.

"Ship ahoy, and in trouble!" Mrs. Mabrity shouted.

The Fairy crew of four was mesmerized by the sight of a ship, with tattered sails clinging to the masts, tossing and pitching wildly in the perilous sea. With their infrared binoculars they could see a small crew of men desperately holding on to the rudder, trying to keep the ship from capsizing.

"There is no light to guide them," Mrs. Mabrity moaned. "Oh where are those boys with the whale oil? If I go to find them I will never get all the lanterns cleaned! Then the lights will not shine brightly enough to prevent disaster."

The Fairy crew snapped to attention and Enjella zapped the buckets to full size. Just then the boys burst up the stairs.

"Thank the heavens boys, you've come in time to help me save this ship. For without this light the boat will crash on the reef and surely the crew will perish!"

"But Ma," puffed Zachary, "We were not able to bring. . ."

"The buckets flew up the stairs themselves!" wheezed Thaddeus.

"That's right my son, when you are doing a good deed, and fulfill-ing your responsibilities, the work seems to do itself. But tonight we all need to turn to, and work our hardest. The ship is in grave danger, and . . ." Mrs. Mabrity stopped short and rubbed her eyes. The boys stared.

From one of the full buckets, two ladles were moving toward two lanterns! As they watched, the ladles poured whale oil into the lanterns' reservoir. Two sparks of light were twinkling over the buckets.

"'Tis a devil of a storm playing heavenly tricks on me eyes!" said Mrs. Mabrity. "But there is no time to waste wondering how the good Lord is working this miracle, we surely must do our part." She grabbed a bucket and another ladle and starting filling another lantern.

"Make haste, boys! Fill two lanterns! Then go find your sisters. We may be able to save this ship after all, and then we must save ourselves! Gather the family and bring them to the lighthouse. I'm afeared this wind is ferocious enough to blow our cabin away."

"Oh no!" the words escaped from Abigail's lips. Before anyone could even remind her not to shout she flew down the stairs (literally, for she was still wearing the Fairy wings) and out into the night.

Mrs. Mabrity got one lantern burning!

Bennett looked at the two Fairies. "Where on earth could she have gone?" he asked.

"To save the other children," Enjella knew. "You two stay here and keep helping," she whispered quickly, "Those boys are worse than no help at all." They all turned their heads to see the two boys arguing over how to dip the ladle into the oil and pour it into the lamp. One shoved the other and the punching began again.

"That ship is not out of danger yet," said Alicia, lifesavers again hanging from her hair, "Aye aye, Captain, we are on deck."

Enjella zipped down the stairs in pursuit of Abigail.

CHAPTER ELEVEN

Winging It

The door at the bottom of the lighthouse was ajar and Enjella flew out the opening. Immediately, the wind blew her back in.

Enchanted Elbows! she thought, this is no night to fly. How in the heavens can Abigail get to the cabin?

Where in the heavens is she?

"I would just zap myself to the house, but then how would I find Abigail?" she muttered. Enjella tapped her feet with her wand and suction cups appeared on the bottom of her shoes. She attached herself to the wall of the lighthouse and crept outside. Her wings and her dress blew straight out behind her. Even with the suction cups the wind threatened to send her tumbling backwards. She reached her hands toward the side of the wall and clung with all her might.

In spite of her infrared binocular vision, she could see no sign of Abigail in the darkness.

She took a step out further on the side of the lighthouse wall. A fierce gust of wind blew her back inside the door, suction cups and all.

"This is getting me nowhere fast," she said. "Poor Abigail, afraid of the hurricane, out there all alone, trying to rescue the children. I have to find her and help!

"Take me to Abigail," she said, and tapped herself with her wand. Instantly she was transported to the door of the light keeper's cabin. Abigail was just outside, struggling against the wind to open it.

"You brave girl. How did you get here?" Enjella cried.

"I took Giant Steps!" Abigail shouted. "I got here in minutes!"

But Enjella could not hear her, the wind whipped the words out of her mouth and they were lost in the wild night.

"No matter, what is your plan?" shouted Enjella.

"To rescue the children and bring them to the lighthouse," shouted Abigail, trying desperately to stand straight and keep the rain and her long hair out of her eyes.

"I know! But how?" asked Enjella.

"Walk them back," replied Abigail.

"But you are invisible, how are you going to do that?" asked Enjella.

The storm ripped the words out of Abigail's mouth and Enjella again could not hear her.

"This is silly," said Enjella, "and dangerous!"

She tapped Abigail with her wand. Instantly, they were both inside the house.

"I'm still thinking of a plan," Abigail was shouting, and her voice suddenly boomed through the house. The cry of a baby in the next room stopped in the middle of a sob. Small feet hit the floor and scurried to the door.

A girl about Abigail's age appeared in the doorway, dressed in a home-spun dress covered by a big pinafore, carrying a red-faced baby on her hip.

"Oh Mary, 'tis not thy brothers come to help us, it is nothing but the wind!" she exclaimed. The baby scrunched up her face and let out a big howl.

"Hush, hush," said the girl. "Mother will return from her duties, post haste, to be certain."

The baby was not persuaded. Abigail and Enjella just hovered, watching the baby cry and the girl try to calm her, distracted from hatching an escape plan.

Enjella tapped Abigail into another room. "We have to come up with a plan and I don't want that girl to hear us. Come on, think."

"Can't you just zap us all into the lighthouse?" asked Abigail.

"Honey, if I could just randomly use my magic, I would save the world! But there are some things even Fairies are not allowed to do."

"But you can fly me, why can't you fly her?"

"She lived in a time when there were no Elbow Fairies, only Tooth Fairies, and all they could do was zap baby teeth into silver coins. But I digress!"

"Whatever that means," Abigail muttered. "I guess we just have to get them to safety the old fashioned way. Make me visible and my normal size and I will walk them to the lighthouse."

Enjella fluttered her wings and looked upset. Little sparkles flew from her hair as she tried to think of another way to help the two stranded girls.

She snapped out her wings in frustration. "I've got nothing!" she confessed. "We just have to 'wing it'!"

She zapped Abigail back to her regular, visible size, her wings disappearing in the process. Enjella twinkled along as Abigail walked into the next room.

The baby again stopped in mid sob and the older girl caught her breath as Abigail appeared, accompanied by a twinkling spark of light.

"Who are you and why are you attired in such a strange fashion?" asked the girl. "Have you lost your pinafore in the storm?"

Abigail smiled and said, "It is very complicated to explain, but I have come to help you."

"Can I get you one of my old frocks to cover your pantaloons?" asked Nicolasa, shocked to see a girl wearing pants.

"Thank you, but we don't have time!" said Abigail. "I have been sent to help you get to the lighthouse."

"I am not permitted to go with you. Mother left very clear instructions to stay here and take care of baby Mary unless she sends Zachary for me." Nicolasa answered very politely, trying not to stare at Abigail's "pantaloons."

"But your mother wants you to come to the lighthouse! She is afraid that the storm will be so fierce that the wind will blow your cabin down."

"Mother's instructions were clear!" repeated the girl simply. "Unless the heavens have come to help me, I must not disobey Mother."

"Aha!" said Abigail. She turned to Enjella, "Zap me another pair of wings," she whispered to the twinkle next to her.

Enjella was just about to argue and remind her that the wind was too fierce for flying when she realized what Abigail was thinking. Quickly she zapped her some beautiful angel wings and a long flowing gown.

"The heavens HAVE sent me," said Abigail, "along with your mother! More accurately, she tried to send Zachary but he was busy helping your brother Thaddeus fill the lighthouse lamps. Your mother has to save a ship floundering at sea in the storm."

"The heavens must be helping if my two brothers are working toward the same purpose!"

Abigail and Nicolasa giggled. "Yes! I noticed your brothers did not get along very well! That is why I am to guide you and your baby sister to the lighthouse."

"You are my Guardian Angel!" the girl exclaimed.

"Why didn't I think of that!" said Abigail. "Oh, I mean: Of course! Grab your coat and let's get going, it is not getting any calmer out there."

"What strange discourse," said Nicolasa. "However, I will don my cloak and we will away, post haste."

Water started to seep into the room from under the front door!

"Hurry, hurry!" urged Abigail and Enjella.

CHAPTER TWELVE

Magical Miracles

The baby watched with round eyes as Abigail tried to put her chubby arms into a sweater. It was so hard to keep her from wriggling! Abigail looked imploringly at Enjella.

A quick tap of Enjella's wand had the sweater on, and buttoned up to the baby's chin, all warm and cozy.

Water started flowing in faster and the room was flooding all the way back to the kitchen.

Nicolasa frantically finished buttoning her boots.

Abigail picked up her ears said, "What is that?"

"I heard nothing," said the girl.

"That's just it," said Abigail, "where is the noise of the wind?

"It must be the eye of the hurricane," whispered Enjella.

Abigail threw open the door and more water gushed into the house.

Somehow, though, the outside world was calmer. The rain still came down in sheets, but Enjella was right, there suddenly was no wind.

Abigail put her arm and wing around the girl who clutched baby Mary. Ducking their heads against the driving rain, they walked slowly and steadily toward the lighthouse.

"I've got it," said Enjella, and tapped Abigail's angel wings.

Both girls could now open their eyes without being pelted with rain. "I made them waterproof," giggled Enjella.

Abigail smiled and they kept slowly walking.

Suddenly the wind picked up again and baby Mary started to cry and fidget in Nicolasa's arms.

"Just a little bit further," urged Abigail to Nicolasa and Mary. Mary drew in her breath and then sobbed even louder. Between the wind and the rain and her crying baby sister, Nicolasa struggled to move ahead.

A big gust of wind knocked them all to their knees. Abigail drew her wings around them tighter to protect them and reached out her hand to help Nicolasa regain her feet. Enjella buzzed in her ear.

"We have to do something about the baby," Enjella whispered. "Nicolasa isn't strong enough to carry her any more."

"May I hold your sister?" asked Abigail in a soothing voice.

"Surely that would be most beneficial," gulped Nicolasa, but as she tried to hand her sister to Abigail, the baby screamed louder. Clutching Nicolasa and clinging to her arms, baby Mary screamed and thrashed so violently she knocked Nicolasa over again.

"We have to think of something!" shouted Enjella.

The safety of the lighthouse seemed unreachable.

"I have it! A spell you were allowed to do even when you were only a Tooth Fairy! Use your Fairy dust to lull her to sleep with a sweet dream!" whispered Abigail.

"You are a genius!" whispered back the twinkling spark of Enjella and instantly the baby smiled and relaxed her body.

Abigail scooped her up in her arms as the baby's heavy eyelids closed. Sound asleep and happy, the baby snuggled into Abigail's shoulder with a sigh.

Nicolasa struggled to her feet. The wind howled and blew and the rain drove down so hard it started to drip on the heads of the girls through the protective waterproof angel wings.

The girls focused on putting one foot in front of the other until at last they were at the door of the lighthouse.

Abigail opened her wings further and the tips touched the walls. She tried to shield them with her wings as they tugged on the door.

But the door would not budge. Wearily they leaned against the wall of the lighthouse, the wind now whipping Abigail's wings and threatening to knock them over again.

Suddenly the door burst open by itself!

"Thank you Enjella!" whispered Abigail.

"Oh Lord, praise and thanksgiving!" said Nicolasa and they stumbled through the door. With renewed energy, she grabbed her happily snoring sister from Abigail, and ran up the spiral staircase to the top of the lighthouse.

Abigail smiled with relief.

Enjella tapped her with her wand and made Abigail invisible.

"Me bairns are safe, praise Jesus!" shouted Mrs. Mabrity. "Your guardian angel must have been with you to get you through this storm."

"Yes Mother, she was," said Nicolasa. "In fact she is right behind me!"

The two boys stopped arguing in mid punch and looked expectantly toward the stairway. Mrs. Mabrity wiped her hands on her apron and turned around.

Invisible Abigail and tiny twinkling Enjella floated silently up the stairs. Alicia and Bennett held their breath. No one even felt the breeze.

"Alas, my child I fear this trauma is afflicting your reasoning," Mrs. Mabrity smiled lovingly at her daughter and caught baby Mary up in her arms and gave her a kiss.

"Mother, I am not speaking falsely! My guardian angel is fair of face and of an age like mine. Surely, at first I thought she was a product of the devil, dressed only in her pantaloons. . ."

Thaddeus shouted with laughter and Zachary poked him in the ribs.

Mrs. Mabrity grinned. "Now fret you not, dearest daughter. When we do our best to overcome insurmountable obstacles and help each other with a smile, something magical happens!

"Finally, all our lanterns are full and shining brightly. When the rain abates, even for an instant, our beam is visible for miles. In the calm of the eye of the storm, my spyglass showed no sign of the ship we saw in danger of wrecking on the treacherous rocks. I reckon it is past us now. With help from the Lord they are in safe harbor or at least in a calmer part of the bay.

"Our duties fulfilled, we can keep safe here and weather the storm while our splendid lighthouse guides any ship unfortunate enough to be out in this hurricane.

"Now let us settle ourselves a wee bit," Mrs. Mabrity continued cheerfully as she opened a storage box and pulled out two comforters and a nice warm shawl. "We have four hours before I must again trim the wicks, just sufficient time to fashion a wee surprise for you. What say this family to a steaming mug of hot chocolate?"

"It would seem more like a cup of magic, Mother," said Nicolasa happily.

The boys clapped and gave each other a bear hug.

In the bustle of the children's happy surprise at the treat, and Mrs. Mabrity's cheerful activity, the two Fairies tapped the invisible children with their wands and in an instant they were back in the 21st century, sitting on top of their luxuriously modern, warm, dry beds.

"NOOOOO!" said Abigail. "I want to stay and see what happens. Are they going to be ok? How bad is the rest of the hurricane?"

"Fiddlesticks!" said Bennett. "I wanted to stay and have hot chocolate."

"Fiddlesticks?" asked Abigail. "Where did you learn that word?"

"That's what Thaddeus said again and again to Zachary! What does it mean anyway?"

"It's the nickname for the bow for a violin!" laughed Enjella. "I see this little adventure has provided SOME education!"

"Commander, we have accomplished our mission," saluted Alicia, wearing a full Navy uniform.

"In spite of her drama, Alicia is right! Every human needs a little magic in his or her life and tonight our magic had a dual purpose. We not only helped some people in need, but we re-lived an exciting moment in history and meet some real-life heroes. We got to experience how people used the resources and technology they had available to perform miraculous feats and save lives."

"Now I know why they invented radar!" said Bennett.

"And better ways to predict the weather, so people don't go out in severe storms," chimed in Abigail.

"That's right!" shouted Alicia, as bells and whistles sounded and streamers unfurled over them, out of thin air. "Congratulations! You both go to the head of the class!"

"Humans live in a much safer world today, that we take for granted, because smart people have figured out ways to invent technology that saves us from these dangers," Enjella smiled at them.

"But don't keep us in suspense! What happened to the Mabritys?" pleaded Abigail.

"How bad was the hurricane?" shouted Bennett.

"Hold your horses there," said Alicia, and cowboy hats appeared on everyone's heads.

Enjella giggled, "More questions! How wonderful!"

"The Mabritys survive the storm and the only casualty is the floor in the light keeper's house. It was covered with mud when the water receded and poor Nicolasa had to scrub the whole thing by herself."

"Why didn't Mrs. Mabrity make her brothers help?" asked Abigail.

"They were supposed to, but they spent the whole time arguing over who got to use the mop and who had to fetch the water."

The children laughed and the Fairies did somersaults in the air. A yawn escaped from Bennett.

"My goodness, look at the time!" said Enjella, clocks and numbers appearing all over the walls.

"But it is only one minute after you first came to get us!" said Abigail.

"How can that be?" asked Bennett. "That adventure took way longer than one minute!"

"Look Kiddo, of course it did! But we didn't want your parents to miss you, and since we were messing with time anyway, I thought we would make sure you did not lose any of your beauty rest!" said Alicia,

ZZZZZZs appearing in her hair, and the sound of snoring emanating faintly from the crown of her head.

"We are not tired," said Abigail.

"We could not possibly fall asleep," said Bennett, simultaneously.

Alicia and Enjella put their hands on their hips.

"As your Elbow Fairies we advise there is a strict protocol we must follow in order to share our magic with you!" said Enjella.

"Huh?" both children said, looking confused.

Rulers appeared in Alicia's hair and her wand turned into a yardstick.

"There are rules we have to follow or we can't come see you every night!" Alicia said.

"Ohhhhhh!" the children sighed, and Alicia zapped the tops of their heads and light bulbs appeared.

The children giggled. Enjella lifted them up with her wand and pulled down the blankets. They were floated down under the covers, still giggling.

"But we really are much too excited about our fun adventure to sleep!" said Abigail.

"I am certainly not tired," said Bennett.

"We will see about that!" said Alicia and Enjella together, raising their wands and getting ready to tap their elbows.

"Wait!" said Abigail. "Before you zap us to sleep, tell me, will we see you tomorrow night?"

"Absolutely," said Alicia.

"I'll bring you magic every night," promised Enjella, "or my name isn't Enjella the Elbow Fairy!

"It's just like Mrs. Mabrity says, when people help each other with a smile on their face something magic happens!"

In a twinkling swirl of rainbow colors, the children fell asleep, still smiling.

Giggling, the two Fairies gave the WINGS UP sign and disappeared amid a shower of sparkles.